A Note to Parents

Welcome to REAL KIDS READERS, a series of phonics-based
books for children who are beginning to read. In the class-
room, educators use phonics to teach children how to sound
out unfamiliar words, providing a firm foundation for reading
skills. At home, you can use REAL KIDS READERS to reinforce
and build on that foundation, because the books follow the
same basic phonic guidelines that children learn in school.

Of course the best way to help your child become a good reader
is to make the experience fun—and REAL KIDS READERS do that,
too. With their realistic story lines and lively characters, the
books engage children's imaginations. With their clean design
and sparkling photographs, they provide picture clues that help
new readers decipher the text. The combination is sure to enter-
tain young children and make them truly want to read.

REAL KIDS READERS have been developed at three distinct
levels to make it easy for children to read at their own pace.

- LEVEL 1 is for children who are just beginning to read.
- LEVEL 2 is for children who can read with help.
- LEVEL 3 is for children who can read on their own.

A controlled vocabulary provides the framework at each level.
Repetition, rhyme, and humor help increase word skills.
Because children can understand the words and follow the
stories, they quickly develop confidence. They go back to each
book again and again, increasing their proficiency and sense of
accomplishment, until they're ready to move on to the next
level. The result is a rich and rewarding experience that will
help them develop a lifelong love of reading.

For my friend Marcia
—M. F.

Special thanks to After the Stork, Albuquerque, NM; Hanna Andersson, Portland, OR; and Lands' End, Dodgeville, WI, for supplying clothing.

Produced by DWAI / Seventeenth Street Productions, Inc.

Library of Congress Cataloging-in-Publication Data

Finch, Margo.
   The lunch bunch / by Margo Finch ; photography by Dorothy Handelman.
         p.   cm. — (Real kids readers. Level 2)
   Summary: Three girls eat lunch together and become friends.
   ISBN 0-7613-2005-9 (lib. bdg.). — ISBN 0-7613-2030-X (pbk.)
   [1. Friendship—Fiction. 2. Schools—Fiction.] I. Handelman, Dorothy, ill. II. Title. III. Series.
PZ7.F49566Lu   1998
[E]—dc21   97-31377
                                                                                CIP
                                                                                AC

pbk: 10 9 8 7 6 5 4 3 2
lib: 10 9 8 7 6 5 4 3 2 1

The Lunch Bunch

Margo Finch

Photographs by Dorothy Handelman

M
The Millbrook Press
Brookfield, Connecticut

It is time for lunch.
Meg knows what is in her brown bag.
Mom packs the same thing each day.
It is what Meg likes:
A hard-boiled egg, a roll, fruit, and milk.

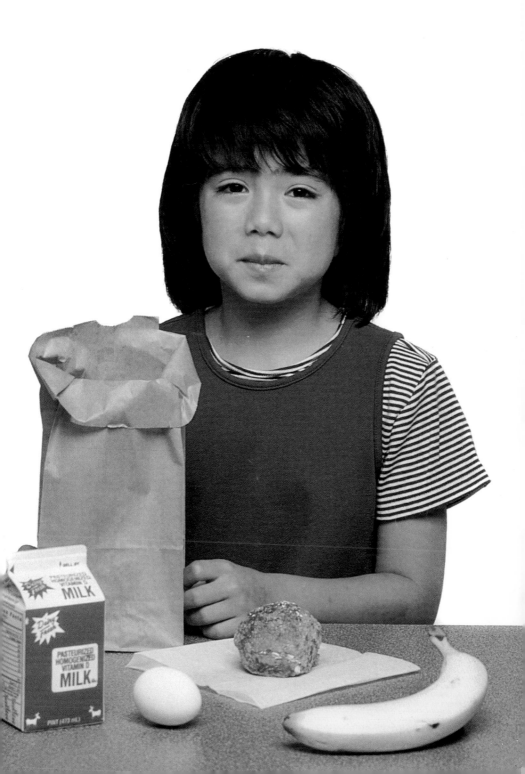

Meg is new at this school.
Where should she sit?
Ann sits with Lee.
They trade parts of their lunch.
It looks like fun.

Meg asks Ann and Lee
if she can sit with them.
They say OK.

Ann has ham.
Lee has cheese with holes.
Ann trades her ham for Lee's cheese.

Meg wishes she could trade too.
But she feels shy.
So she does not ask.

That night Meg talks to Mom.
She says she wants cheese for lunch—
cheese with holes.
Then Ann might trade with her.
Mom says OK.
She is glad that Meg wants to try
a new lunch.
But Ann is not at school the next day.
She has a bad cold.

At lunch Meg sits with Lee.
They both have cheese with holes!
It would be dumb to trade.
So Meg eats cheese for lunch.

It tastes good.
But you can't crack it
on your head like an egg.
Meg tells Lee, and they both laugh.

Ann is still home with her cold
the next day.
Meg has cheese for lunch again.
And this time Lee has an egg!

She asked her mom for it
so she and Meg could trade.
Lee gets Meg's cheese with holes.
Meg gets Lee's egg.

Meg cracks the egg on her head.
Lee says that looks like fun.
Meg and Lee make a plan.

The next day, they won't trade.
They will both bring eggs
and crack them on their heads.

The next day, Ann is back.
At lunch she sits with Meg and Lee.
Meg and Lee take out their eggs.
They crack them on their heads.

Meg and Lee talk and laugh.
Ann does not say much.
And she does not laugh.

Lee has grapes to trade.
Meg and Ann both want them.
Lee says Meg can have them.
Meg reaches for the grapes—
and hits Ann's milk.
Oh, no! What a mess!
Ann's jeans are all wet.
Meg and Lee try to clean up the milk.
But Ann is mad.

The next day, Ann does not sit
with Lee and Meg.
Lee is quiet.
She keeps turning to look at Ann.

Meg feels bad for Lee.
She wants to have Lee for her friend.
But she knows Lee likes Ann too.

Meg has an idea.
That night she talks it over with Mom.
Mom says she will help.

Meg gets out her art stuff.
While she works,
she plans what to say to Ann.

The next day, Meg asks Ann
to sit with her and Lee.
At first Ann says no.
Then she says yes.

She sits down with them.
She is not mad.
Meg can tell that Lee is glad.
Meg is glad too.

Meg opens her brown bag
and takes out three eggs.
One has Ann's name on it.
One has Lee's. And one has Meg's.

Meg and Lee show Ann
how to crack her egg on her head.
Then Meg takes out a bunch of grapes.
They all have a great time at lunch.

Now Meg has two lunches she likes:
Hard-boiled egg and cheese with holes.
And she has two friends.
Meg eats lunch with Ann and Lee each day.
Some days they trade. Some days they share.

They have made up a name.
They are The Lunch Bunch.
But they are not just friends at lunch.
They are friends all day long.

Phonic Guidelines

Use the following guidelines to help your child read the words in *The Lunch Bunch*.

Short Vowels

When two consonants surround a vowel, the sound of the vowel is usually short. This means you pronounce *a* as in apple, *e* as in egg, *i* as in igloo, *o* as in octopus, and *u* as in umbrella. Short-vowel words in this story include: *bad, bag, but, can, fun, gets, ham, has, hits, mad, Meg, Mom, not, sit, wet.*

Consonant Blends

When two or more different consonants are side by side, they usually blend to make a combined sound. In this story, words with consonant blends include: *ask, bring, cold, crack, glad, help, milk, next, plan.*

Double Consonants

When two identical consonants appear side by side, one of them is silent. Double-consonant words in this story include: *egg, mess, roll, still, stuff, tell, will.*

R-Controlled Vowels

When a vowel is followed by the letter *r*, its sound is changed by the *r*. In this story, words with *r*-controlled vowels include: *art, for, hard, her, parts.*

Long Vowel and Silent E

If a word has a vowel and ends with an *e*, usually the vowel is long and the *e* is silent. Long vowels are pronounced the same way as their alphabet names. In this story, words with a long vowel and silent *e* include: *grapes, holes, home, like, made, name, same, takes, tastes, time, trade.*

Double Vowels

When two vowels are side by side, usually the first vowel is long and the second vowel is silent. Double-vowel words in this story include: *clean, day, each, feels, jeans, say.*

Diphthongs

Sometimes when two vowels (or a vowel and a consonant) are side by side, they combine to make a diphthong—a sound that is different from long or short vowel sounds. Diphthongs are: *au, aw, ew, oi, oy, ou, ow.* In this story, words with diphthongs include: *boiled, brown, new, out.*

Consonant Digraphs

Sometimes when two different consonants are side by side, they make a digraph that represents a single new sound. Consonant digraphs are: *ch, sh, th, wh.* In this story, words with digraphs include: *both, bunch, cheese, each, lunch, much, that, them, they, thing, this, what, where, while, wishes, with.*

Silent Consonants

Sometimes when two different consonants are side by side, one of them is silent. In this story, words with silent consonants include: *dumb, knows, talk.*

Sight Words

Sight words are those words that a reader must learn to recognize immediately—by sight—instead of by sounding them out. They occur with high frequency in easy texts. Sight words not included in the above categories are: *a, an, and, asks, at, be, does, friend, good, have, if, in, is, it, kind, look, new, no, of, oh, she, should, so, the, their, to, up, would, your.*